The Ugly Duckling

tiger tales

To Jess . . . and to all the ducklings at
Boston Public Garden ~ M. A.

For Yasmin and Baldrik ~ S. E.

tiger tales
5 River Road, Suite 128, Wilton, CT 06897
Published in the United States 2017
Originally published in Great Britain 2014
by Little Tiger Press
Text copyright © 2014 Little Tiger Press
Illustrations copyright © 2014 Sue Eastland
ISBN-13: 978-1-68010-046-4
ISBN-10: 1-68010-046-7
Printed in China
LTP/1400/1680/0916
For more insight and activities,
visit us at www.tigertalesbooks.com

The Ugly Duckling

adapted by Mara Alperin

Illustrated by Sue Eastland

tiger tales

It was a sunny spring morning on the farm. Mother Duck was watching her eggs.

"Come quickly!" she called to the other animals. "My eggs are beginning to hatch!"

Crack! Crack! Crack! Crack!

Out tumbled four perfect little ducklings. They were soft and fluffy and yellow.

"Cheep!
Cheep!"
chirped the baby ducklings.
And Mother Duck gave them
a big hug.

But there was ONE egg left. It was bigger than the others, and strangely speckled. Then it began to crack open. Out popped . . .

two funny feet,

two waving wings,

and one bumpy beak.

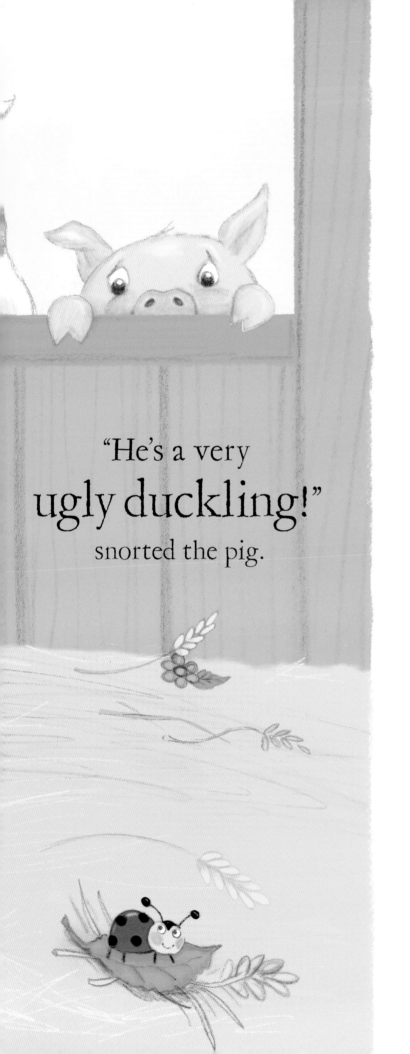

"He's a very
ugly duckling!"
snorted the pig.

"Hush!" scolded Mother Duck.
"He's my baby, and I love him.

Now come along, my little
ducklings — it's time for your
first swimming lesson."

Mother Duck
   marched toward the pond,
      and four little ducklings
         skipped along behind.

"Wait for me!" called the
   ugly duckling. But he tripped over
      his funny feet, and . . .

Thump!

Bump!

Thump!

Bump!

...he tumbled into the other little ducklings.

How clumsy!

"It's okay," said Mother Duck. "Now, into the water like good little ducklings."

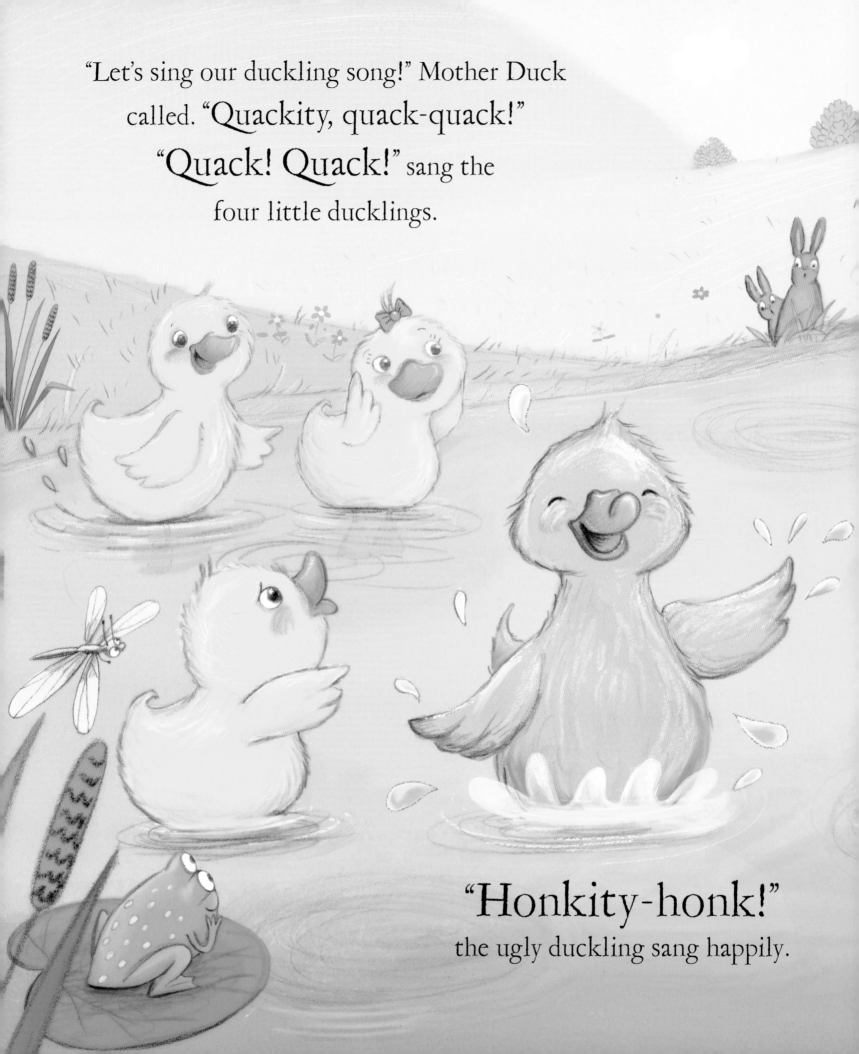

"Let's sing our duckling song!" Mother Duck
called. "Quackity, quack-quack!"
"Quack! Quack!" sang the
four little ducklings.

"Honkity-honk!"
the ugly duckling sang happily.

"What was that?" asked the horse.
"You don't sing like a duckling!"
"Be nice!" said Mother Duck.
"He'll learn in time."

But the ugly duckling didn't learn. And all summer long the other animals teased him when he . . .

got stuck in things . . .

tripped and fell . . .

No matter how hard he tried, the ugly duckling just didn't fit in.

"Go away!" quacked the other little ducklings.
"You're noisy and messy, and you ruin our fun!"
Just then, they heard Mother Duck
calling for them.

"Not you!" shouted
the ducklings.

And off they pranced . . .
leaving the ugly duckling behind.

"Why doesn't anyone want to play with me?" sighed the ugly duckling.

"No time to play!" said a mole, popping his head up. "I'm digging a new tunnel for the winter."

"Can I help?" asked the ugly duckling. And he poked his bumpy beak underground.

"Where are you, my little one?" quacked Mother Duck. "We can't wait any longer – it's time to fly south for the winter."

"I'm coming!" cried the ugly duckling. "Wait for me!"

But the ugly duckling was stuck in the tunnel, and Mother Duck didn't hear him.

The ugly duckling wriggled and wiggled,
and he pushed and he pulled, until ...

POP!

At last he was free.

But it was too late – they had
left without him.

"Oh, no," sniffed the ugly duckling.
"I'll never catch up with them now.
I'm all alone."

The days and
nights grew colder,
and the ugly duckling
huddled in the
hollow of an old
oak tree.

And as the snowflakes fell,
he curled up in his long wings
and dreamed of sunny days and
games in the meadow.

At last, the sun peeked out,
and the frozen pond
began to thaw.

Then one day, a beautiful
swan glided across the
sparkling water.

"Who's there?" called the swan. "Come out and play!"

"I can't," whispered the ugly duckling. "I'm too funny-looking, and everybody laughs at me."

The ugly duckling peeked out from behind the cattails. "I wish I could go swim with her," he said. "But I'm too ugly to be her friend!" And he gave a little sob.

"I won't laugh," promised the swan. "I don't care what you look like."

So the ugly duckling took a deep breath, and stepped into the pond . . . .

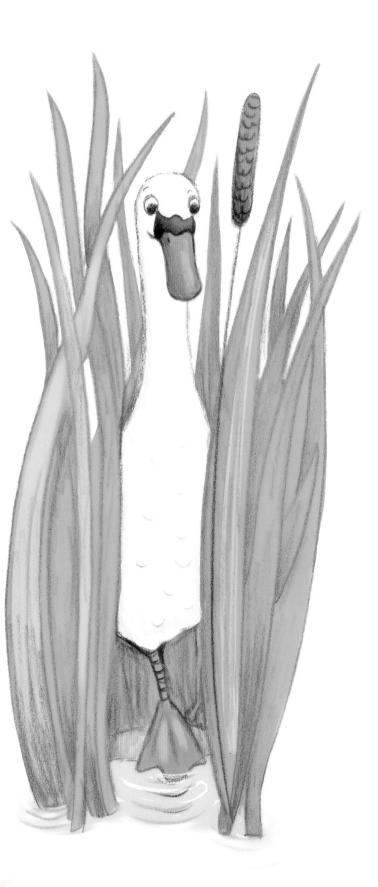

"You're beautiful!" exclaimed the swan. "Look!"

So he looked down at his reflection . . . and saw that she was right!

The ugly duckling had grown into a swan!
A **beautiful**, **elegant** swan, with dazzling
white feathers and a long,
graceful neck.

So they played together all day long.
He was very happy, because at last,
he had found a **friend**.

Mara Alperin

Mara has adapted all of the books
in the My First Fairy Tales series, which also includes
*Little Red Riding Hood, Goldilocks and the Three Bears,
Jack and the Beanstalk, The Three Billy Goats Gruff,
Chicken Little, The Gingerbread Man, Rumpelstiltskin,
The Three Little Pigs,* and *The Elves and the Shoemaker.* As a child,
she loved listening to fairy tales and then retelling the stories
to her family and friends.
Mara lives in London, England.

Sue Eastland

Sue works as a children's book illustrator and sometimes author from her
studio overlooking her yard in the small but merry city of Wakefield,
England. She lives with her husband and daughter, who are always
thinking up "brilliant" ideas for stories and characters. Between working
and waiting for the muse, she can be found walking her Sheltie, Bilbo,
closely followed by her two cats, Maurice and Maisy.